*For my mother, of course...*
Alice.


*For Liliane and Martin, my parents.*
Celia.

General Manager: Gauthier Auzou
Senior Editor: Florence Pierron
English Version Editor: Nelson Yomtov
Graphics and layout: Annaïs Tassone
Original title: *Pierre la lune*
© Éditions Auzou, Paris (France),
2011 (English version)
ISBN: 978-2-7338-1940-1

Printed and bound in China, 2011

# Peter

## and the
## Moon

By Alice Briere-Haquet
Illustrated by Celia Chauffrey

AUZOU

This is the story of a little boy named Peter, who,
Because he is small, is not very tall.

This story is also about his mother, who is not small,
Because she is naturally tall.
Not only is she very thoughtful,
But she is also very beautiful.
Of course, she is very intelligent
As well as being very elegant.

Peter, who is not very tall,
Would like to give his mother
The most wonderful gift of all:
Just as wonderful as she,
And which really has to be.
Just as big as her heart,
A bright light in the dark.
Just as warm as her embrace,
And full of happiness.

This ideal gift from afar
Can only be found among the stars.
We have only one mother,
The moon is the very least we can offer her!

But how is it possible to give such a gift?
It is a challenge that is really quite difficult.
Especially when you are not very tall,
And even harder when you are rather small.

The little boy gets an idea and asks his father
who is standing near,

"Daddy, let me climb on your shoulders, please,
And I promise to give you a piece!"

His father says okay
And helps him climb up right away.

But even then, after all,
The little boy is still too small.

The little boy then asks his cousins,

"Let us climb on your shoulders, please,
And I promise to give you a piece!"

And so each cousin takes up their position,
With Peter's father at the top, in addition.

But even then, after all,
The little boy is still too small.

The little boy then
Asks his neighbours,

"Let us climb on your shoulders, please,
And I promise to give you a piece!"

And so each neighbour
takes up their position,
With Peter's father at the top,
in addition.

But even then, and after all,
The little boy is still too small.

The little boy then asks people from farther away,

"Let us climb on your shoulders, please,
And I promise to give you a piece!"

At the bottom are the people from farther away,
The neighbours place themselves without delay.
Each cousin takes up their original position,
With Peter's father at the top, in addition.

But the little boy realizes that there are so many persons,
Should he catch the moon, he is absolutely certain,
That his mother's part will be so small,
It will be a very small part of nothing at all!

Peter has had quite enough.
He is disappointed, annoyed, and quite fed up.
His frustration and anger are both as such,
That he stamps his feet and storms off
in a huff!

The little boy goes off on his way,
In the hope of finding someone who may
Lend him a ladder or giant set of steps,
Or even a fishing rod that could be of some help.

For hours Peter walks and walks,
Without coming to a halt.
For days he treks and treks,
Without taking any breaks.
For almost a month, he keeps up his step,
Without having any rest.
And he has walked so far,
And covered such a distance,
That he has traveled the world,
Much to his amazement!

So very far has he walked alone,
But in the distance, he can see his home.

The little boy is quite relieved,
For he is beginning to tire and he feels pains in his feet.

Peter sees many people who are waiting for him:
His father, his cousins, and the neighbours, of course.
Yet there are other kind people among this array:
The people who have come from farther away!

And the little boy thinks to himself,
That it would only be fair
To give a little piece of the moon to everyone there.

So he climbs on the shoulders of each person,
And he climbs and climbs with great caution.
And because he has grown a little,
This time, the small boy is at last successful!

But very much to his surprise…

The moon is an **incredible** size!

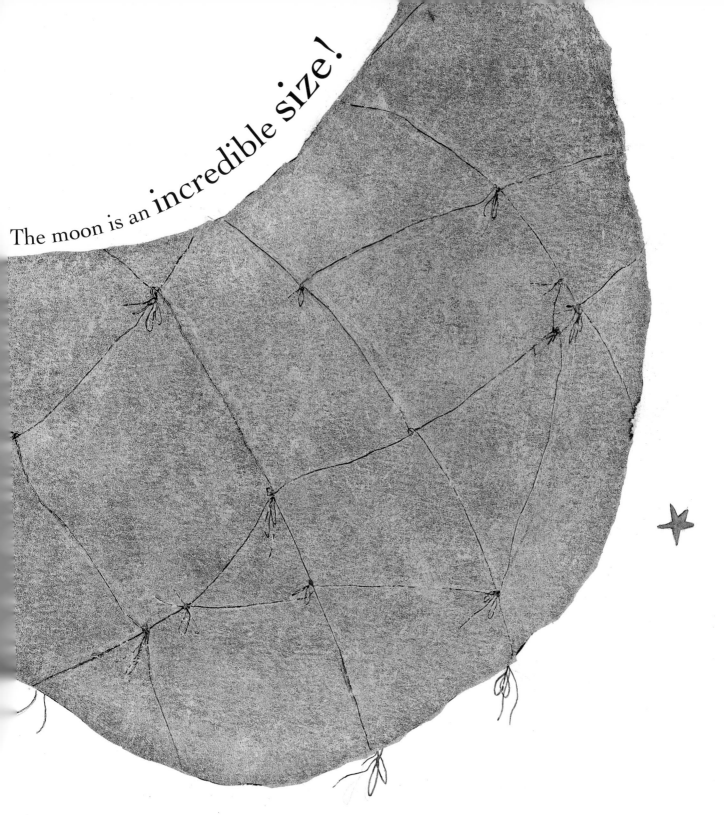

It is big enough for his father and his cousins,
As well as for all his neighbours.
And there is even enough for the other kind people among this array:
The people who have come from farther away!
And if he searches hard enough,
There may even be plenty to offer out,
To the cousins of the neighbours who live next door,
To the people from farther away,
And even for all THEIR mothers, as special as they are,
All may have a piece of moon from among the stars.

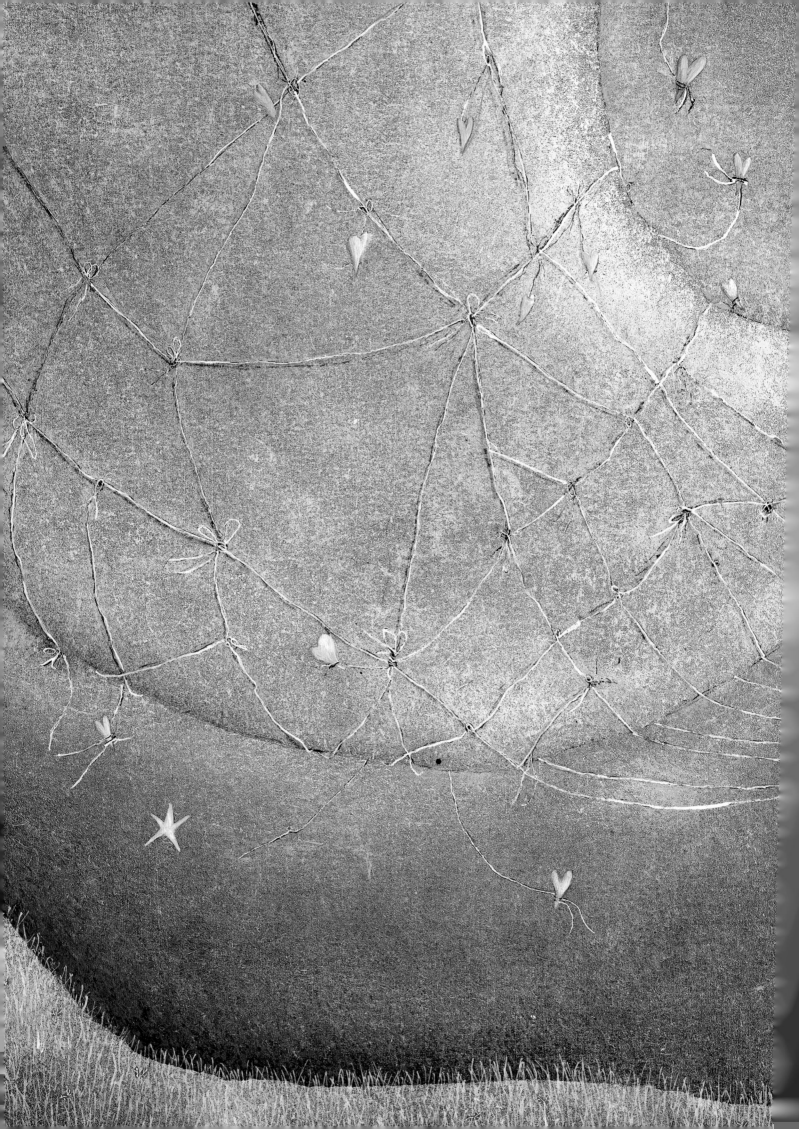

But Peter, who is not very tall,
Gives his mother the prettiest crescent of all.

Because we have only one mother,
The moon is the very least that we can offer her!